Grumpy Cat®

A Is for Awful

A Grumpy Cat ABC Book

By Christy Webster · Illustrated by Steph Laberis

A GOLDEN BOOK · NEW YORK

grumpycats.com
randomhousekids.com
Educators and librarians, for a variety of teaching tools, visit us at RHTeachersLibrarians.com
ISBN 978-0-399-55783-5 (trade)—ISBN 978-0-399-55784-2 (ebook)
Printed in the United States of America
10 9 8 7

Time to learn the alphabet with Grumpy Cat!

"Do we have to?"

A is for ANTS.

"A is for awful. Ants are awful. Everything is awful."

B is for BUTTERFLY.

"Beat it, butterfly.
You're boring me."

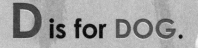

D is for DOG.

"Dear dog, just don't."

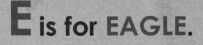

E is for EAGLE.

"Enough already.
Can we just skip to the end?"

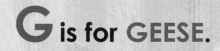

G **is for GEESE.**

"Go away, geese.
You make me gloomy
and grumpy."

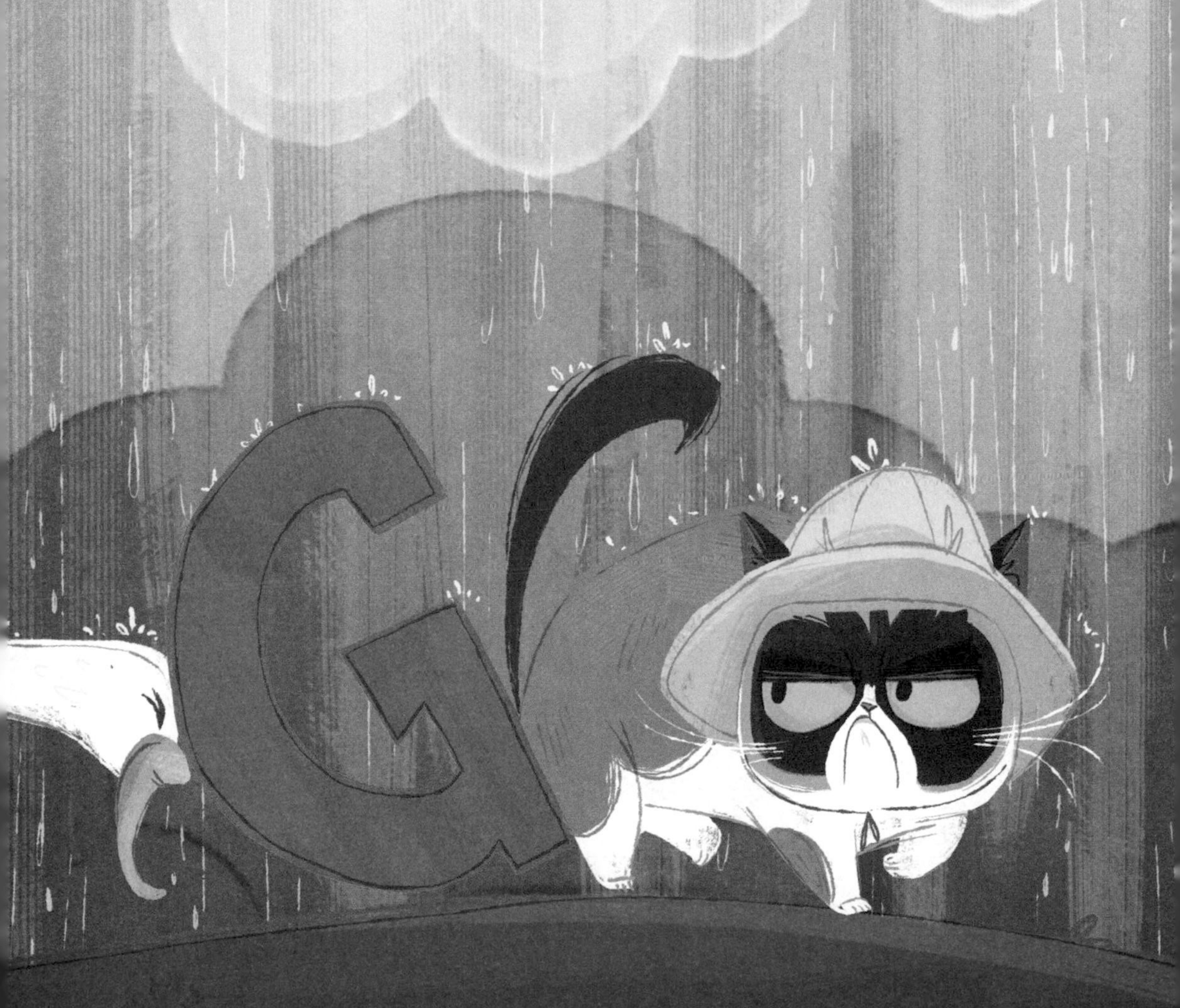

"Got it? Good."

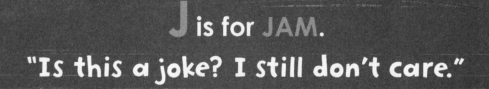

I is for IGUANA.
"I don't care."

J is for JAM.
"Is this a joke? I still don't care."

K is for KITTY.

"Kitty, you're killing me
with kindness."

L is for LADYBUG.

"Ladybug, leave me alone."

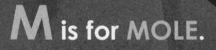

M is for MOLE.

"It's also for mood.
Mine is grumpy."

O is for OWLS.

"Is this over yet?"

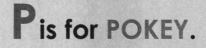

P is for POKEY.

"Please poke me when
this is over."

Q is for QUEEN.

"Buzz away.
Quickly."

R is for RABBITS.

"Really?
This is getting ridiculous."

S is for SQUIRREL.

"Stop it."

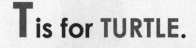

T is for TURTLE.

"Turtle,
the end is too
far away."

U is for UNICORN.

"Ugh! Unicorn, save me from this ugly hat."

V is for VULTURE.

"I'm very tired. Very, very tired."

W is for WORM.

"When can I go to sleep?"

XYZ is for . . .

"Forget it. Goodbye."